Chick:
Lister

Alex Van Tol

ORCA BOOK PUBLISHERS

Published in Canada and the United States in 2020 by Orca Book Publishers.
Previously published in 2015 by Orca Book Publishers
as a softcover (ISBN 9781459810006).
orcabook.com

Library and Archives Canada Cataloguing in Publication
Title: Chick : Lister / Alex Van Tol.
Names: Van Tol, Alex, 1973– author.
Series: Orca currents.
Description: Second edition. | Series statement: Orca currents |
Previously published: Victoria, BC, Canada: Orca Book Publishers, 2015.
Identifiers: Canadiana 20200320904 | ISBN 9781459828223 (softcover)
Classification: LCC PS8643.A63 C45 2020 | DDC jc813/.6—dc23

Library of Congress Control Number: 2020944949

Summary: In this high-interest accessible novel for middle-grade readers, fourteen-year-old
Chick struggles with obsessive-compulsive disorder and his father's expectations.

Orca Book Publishers is committed to reducing the consumption
of nonrenewable resources in the making of our books. We make
every effort to use materials that support a sustainable future.

Orca Book Publishers gratefully acknowledges the support for its publishing programs provided
by the following agencies: the Government of Canada, the Canada Council for the Arts and the
Province of British Columbia through the BC Arts Council and the Book Publishing Tax Credit.

Design by Ella Collier
Cover photography by Getty Images
Author photo by BK Studios

Printed and bound in Canada.

23 22 21 20 • 1 2 3 4

Chapter One

My shoes are too tight. My mouth is dry. And I'm more than a little embarrassed after having pronounced a word wrong in Spanish class. I tried to ask Isobel how old she was, in that weird backward Spanish way. Turns out "How many years do you have?" is just a shade different than "How many anuses do you have?" I'm pretty sure Isobel isn't going to talk to me for the rest of eighth grade. At least it made people laugh.

Now I just want to get home.

Angeline and Maryke pass me in the hallway. "Have a good weekend, Chick." Maryke smiles at me.

I'm not sure if it's a blessing or a curse that my younger brother couldn't pronounce my full name when he was little. And how he got *Chick* from *Tadeusz* beats me. But it stuck.

And it's a good thing. You should hear how people massacre *Tadeusz*. It's supposed to sound like "today-ish." But last year we had a substitute who couldn't work it out. My friends called me *Ta-douche* for a month.

"Thanks, you too." At least they're not cracking butt jokes. That'll come on Monday.

I want to get into my locker so I can grab my books, and then I'm splitting for home. As fast as I can get there. I've got a bit of pressure I need to release.

My fingers tingle as I spin the numbers on my lock. A list of the afternoon's insane events begins to form in my mind.

1. *Jazmin asking me if I'm going to the dance.*
2. *Audrey smiling at me, twice. Twice, people!*
3. *The big A inside a bright red circle on the front page of my math test.*
4. *The anus thing.*

I wish I could write it out instead. *That's* where I find my release. In the writing.

In my mind, I am sitting with a clean, white sheet of paper in front of me. There is a jar of pens. They're all different colors. I look carefully at each one before choosing dark green. I hover there, my imaginary pen poised over the clean page. I savor the anticipation. It's a pleasure-pain feeling, like clamping your teeth together after having your braces tightened.

Back in the real world, I swap a few books, grab my jacket and close my locker. I can't wait to write down all the crazy things from today. And then I'll write a list of all the things I have to do this weekend.

All the things I'm not supposed to forget. I'll explode everything out onto the page. Get it out of my head.

And get my anxiety back under control.

As I sling my bag onto my back, my fantasy is interrupted. "Yo, Chick, wassup?"

I don't even have to look. I'd know Finnian's cheesy hip-hop speak in a crowd of a hundred. My stomach dips and twirls when I see Audrey coming along behind him. She drifts to a stop near my locker, a sweet smile on her face.

My palms start to sweat, and I take a deep breath to steady myself. I am desperate to get home, but I don't want to seem rude or abrupt. Especially to Audrey.

"You heading out?" Fin claps me on the shoulder, even though he has to practically bend down to do it.

I let my knees buckle and bang my head against the locker for effect. Audrey giggles.

"Heading out," I nod, rubbing my forehead. We have a good comic chemistry, Fin and I. It's a good thing we're not debate partners. For the judges' sakes.

I shoot Audrey a smile and follow Finnian through this weird fist-bump-hand-slap-over-the-top-something-or-other that he's been developing. It's lame, but I do it anyway, because it's Finnian. He's my best friend. And everybody loves Finnian. He's a rugby superstar, and girls think he's cute. I mean, they think I'm cute too, but my cute is more of the *Aww, look, he's not even five feet tall* variety.

"You want to go shoot some hoops?"

I look down at myself, then back at Finnian. "You want to go tie two butterflies' tongues together?"

Audrey laughs. I like the way she looks up at me, even though I'm technically shorter than she is. She has this way of dipping her chin down and looking up through her eyelashes. I appreciate it. Maybe if I hung out with Audrey more I wouldn't always be reminded of how short I am.

"Aw, come on, man," Finnian says. "You know how to jump, don't you?"

"I forget."

"Actually..." Audrey interrupts. She pauses in this quiet way she has until we both turn to look at her. "I was going to ask Chick if he could walk me home." She glances at me. I can see she's a little nervous. "There are a couple of things I wanted to talk to you about, for the debate tournament."

Holy schnitzel. Really? I've been struggling to think of a way to ask Audrey to hang out and work on our debate. And here she is, doing it for me.

Finnian rolls his eyes and throws his hands in the air. "Oh, what is *that*? Here I am, the number-one basketball god in the whole school offering you a chance to play. But then a girl shows up, and you're all like 'Yeah, baby, let's *debate!*'"

It's my turn to laugh. As if Finnian would ever truly be upset about this. He knows I'm into Audrey. And he knows I haven't been able to get the ball rolling with her. Well, here it is, rolling. I think.

I look back at Audrey. I search for my tongue, but I must have swallowed it.

Finnian looks from me to Audrey. "Yeah, so um…" He looks from Audrey back to me. "How about I just… leave you kids to it?" He gives a twinkling wave, then spins on his heel and heads for the double doors at the end of the hall. Audrey watches him go.

"You and Finnian are always so funny," she says.

"Thanks." Ah. There's my tongue. Except it feels like it's full of concrete.

"So. Are you headed home now?"

I shrug, but I'm not sure what to say. The idea of walking all the way home with the girl of my dreams makes me feel light-headed. You'd think that's a good thing, right? But it's not. The way my heart is racing, I don't think I can do it. I was already tense when class let out. I'm feeling super anxious, because Audrey is with me.

I don't know if I can hold it together.

Chapter Two

"So…do you want to walk with me then?" Audrey is looking at me a little funny. *Ah, God.*

I run my hand through my hair. Feels like I'm breathing like a locomotive. Are my eyes rolling as wildly as I feel like they are? I feel like the Hulk right before he splits through his clothes. The pressure is that bad. And it's a twenty-minute walk home.

There's no way I'll make it without having a breakdown or a full-blown panic attack.

This is so stupid. Any normal guy would die to walk home with the girl he's been crushing on for five months.

I've got to do something.

I look Audrey straight in the eye. "Yes. Yes, Audrey, I would *love* to walk home with you. Can you hang on a couple minutes?"

She blinks. "Uh, sure?"

"Okay. Thanks. I'll be right back." I turn and bolt for the bathroom down the hall. I'm sure she's wondering what my problem is, but there's nothing I can do about that. Maybe it's better if she thinks I have diarrhea. At least that's only a temporary condition.

In the bathroom, I slam myself into a cubicle and lock the door. My hands shake as I unzip the top pocket of my backpack. I yank out the little red book I keep with me. My book of lists. For emergencies only.

Crazy, right?

I flip the pages as fast as my fingers will go, accidentally tearing one in half in my panic. I find a blank page, whip the pen out of the center coil and wipe my sweaty hand on my jeans. I know I'm breathing hard—I can hear myself. Anyone who comes into the bathroom now is going to think I'm either wickedly constipated or having too much one-handed fun during school hours.

I start with the title. *Crazy Stuff From Today.*

With each item I scribble onto the page, my tension ratchets down a notch. It's a physical relief. Like taking a long pee after having to wait in line for an hour.

I almost laugh at the idea that here I am, in the actual place where people go to pee, but my relief doesn't come from a porcelain bowl. My relief is supplied courtesy of a sheet of lined paper.

I'm still shaking as I finish number ten, but I'm feeling way calmer. I pack my book away and step out of the stall. The empty bathroom echoes around me as I wash my hands and dry them. I glance at myself in the mirror.

It's funny that I can look so normal. No one can see the screwed-up problem inside me.

I pull the door open, arranging my face into a sly grin. I've got a funny one-liner cued up to make Audrey laugh. But when I get out into the hallway, I don't see her anywhere. I look up and down the corridor, but there's no sign of her. Maybe she went to the girls' bathroom.

I wait near a big pot that holds a skinny, leaning fig tree, my hope fading with each passing minute. Does she think I'm a freak for bolting like that?

Oh no. What if she somehow heard me through the door? Slamming cubicle doors and unzipping things and…grunting and…panting?

Oh. My. God. What if she *heard* me? My anxiety

creeps back up until it's squarely in the orange zone.

Again. But, still, I wait.

After ten minutes, I get it.

She's gone.

Chapter Three

We win our soccer game on Saturday afternoon, but that doesn't matter. I know Dad will be upset with me for not scoring more goals. And I'm still upset with myself for flaking out on Audrey yesterday.

Everybody decides to celebrate with a burger at Legacy's. Except me. Dad wouldn't like me changing plans like that. I say goodbye to the team in the parking lot and then lope toward our green

Range Rover. I can almost feel my blood pressure rising as I approach.

The fact that the car is green is a karmic flip-off to the environment. Every one of that monster's eight cylinders guzzles gas like a frat boy in a drinking game. Mom has suggested that maybe we should downsize to something that suits a four-person family a little better.

I could point out to her that we never actually *go* anywhere as a family.

Anyway. Dad isn't into fuel-efficient, environmentally responsible cars. He likes the big truck. And he likes the fact that we live in a big house in one of the nicest neighborhoods in the city. Status symbols matter to him.

He likes people looking up to him. Maybe that's because he's short too.

I hear the doors unlock as I approach the truck. I open the gate and heave my soccer bag inside. Dad's eyes watch me in the rearview mirror. I mentally check off the things he'll want me to report in about. What happened during the game. How debating is going. Whether I've put any more work into my speech for my bar mitzvah.

I close the gate and come around the passenger side, my palms prickling with sweat.

I climb into the leather seat. It's cold. I want to turn on the seat warmer, but it's halfway across the ocean of space between my father and me, so I don't.

"Thanks for coming to watch," I say. Even though he only showed up for the last fifteen minutes. And he was on his phone pretty much the whole time.

He starts the engine. "Nice that you won." As he backs out of the parking spot, my eyes pick out the receding forms of my teammates on their way to lunch.

He clears his throat. The knot in my stomach tightens.

Here it comes.

"You sure do pass that ball around a lot," he says.

Translation: *Why didn't you score more goals?* With Dad, it's all understatement. He's not the kind of guy who'll ask you why you didn't take more shots on goal. He comes at you sideways. Like a crab. You don't see it coming until you feel this huge pinch. He wants me to be a lawyer so bad, but he's the one who thinks all clever and manipulative. My brain just doesn't work like that.

I think about a few possible ways to respond. I frame my answer carefully—but truthfully. "Coach wants us to pass the ball."

And it's true. We spend a lot of time passing in our drills. What soccer team doesn't?

Dad grunts. I know I've picked the right answer, because he doesn't argue.

My feet are sore. These cleats are so uncomfortable. If I were in Mom's car, I'd take them off.

We drive in silence for a few minutes. I wish I could think of something to say. But it's easier not to say anything at all. It's so cold between us that my teeth could chatter.

I could keep the ball to myself when I play. That's what Dad would like me to do. Keep the ball on my own fast feet and pound in the goals. But that doesn't help build team morale. People like having me on the team because I'm not a ball hog. I'm fast and I'm good, and I don't need to always be the one who scores the goals.

But Dad doesn't get that. His approach to life is different from mine. He's a one-man show in his job. Everything he does is for and by himself. He owns a mortgage brokerage. He has a staff of brokers, but they all work for themselves too. There doesn't seem to be much teamwork involved. Just a lot of phone calls and paperwork and handshakes. Closing deals. Racking up the fees. That's what it's about for my dad. Cold hard cash.

He drums on the steering wheel briefly before speaking again.

"Are you spending some time this weekend preparing for your debating competition?"

"You bet," I say.

"Good. You need the practice. What's your topic?" Even though he's asked me twice already.

"Today's kids being overprogrammed."

"And you're arguing for?"

"Against." He's always testing me.

"How many sources have you consulted in your research?"

"I think nine." As soon as I say it, I wish I had dropped the *I think*.

"Sources?"

For a second, I think he's clarifying: *Nine sources?* But then I realize he wants me to list them.

"*The New York Times.* KidsHealth. *The Atlantic.* The Center for Family Wellness." My brain spins like a series of flywheels, scanning back over the names of the magazines and websites I've used. "The Mayo Clinic. National Alliance on Mental Illness." I stretch for one that I know will impress him. "National Institutes of Health and the National Library of Medicine." I'm missing one, but I think I've given him enough for now.

He grunts again.

I release a breath I didn't even know I had been holding.

More silence as we drive. I wonder what my friends would think if they saw me having a conversation with my dad. They wouldn't recognize me as the same guy who cracks jokes that make even the teachers laugh. I brought home a 93 percent average on my report card last term. I made the boys' A soccer team. I win almost all my debates. I babysit. I cook. I even walk Mrs. Pensak's yappy little Yorkshire terrier three times a week.

But it's not enough.

Dad turns onto our street. My heart is pounding now, and I'm feeling dizzy. By the time we pull into the garage, my anxiety is nearly unbearable. I *need* to write. To get away from the stressed-out way he makes me feel. Like I can't ever do anything right.

I wait for him to climb out and close his door before I get out. I heave my soccer bag out of the back and follow him inside, pressing the button to close the garage door behind us.

I unpack, putting my dirty clothes in the laundry basket. I think about the rest of the team, enjoying a burger together. I think about how Audrey took off on me yesterday.

I hear Mom in the kitchen, probably getting lunch ready. Dad has already gone into his study and shut the door.

I hang my empty soccer bag on the hook behind the door. My hands are shaking.

"Chick?"

"Yeah, Mom," I call. I kick off my cleats.

"How was your game, honey?"

"Great, Ma. We won by a point." I hold my cleats over the sink and tap the dirt off. I drop one and pick it up, then drop it again. I force myself to slow down. I place them on the shoe rack. All I can think about is the feel of a pen in my hand.

"That's fabulous!" she exclaims. "Are you coming in here? I need someone to set the table for lunch."

"I'll be there in a sec," I say. My voice breaks, and I clear my throat. "I just gotta run up to my room. Be down in five?"

"Five minutes sounds good, honey."

I take the stairs two at a time.

Chapter Four

I cross the floor to my desk. My mouth almost waters to see the clean white paper neatly stacked on the left-hand corner. A jar of pens sits on the right-hand side.

I pinch a sheet off the paper stack and slide it into place in front of me. I'm strung so tight I can hardly see straight. I try to slow my breathing, but it's no use. I'm like a stone bumping down a hill, picking up speed as I go. I need to feed my addiction.

I jab my hand into the pen jar, not caring whether I pull out a black, blue, green or red. I just need to get started. Is this how it feels to be addicted to drugs? I feel like I'll never be able to get away from this.

I can barely uncap the pen before it hits the paper.

Saturday, September 27th

1. Help Mom set up for lunch
2. Eat lunch

I feel an instant pressure release. Like popping the top of a soda can after it's been shaken.

3. Tidy up
4. Photocopy note-taking sheets for this week's practice debate
5. Read Chapters 6 and 7 in Animal Farm. Margin notes

I savor the calm that washes over me.

6. *Take Wookie for a walk*
7. *Schedule Wookie's walks for the next three weeks*
8. *Write a letter to Bubbe (Butter tarts)*

My pulse slows. I am getting organized. I am getting things under control.

9. *Laundry*
10. *Movie night? Games night? Mom's turn to decide*

Just a couple more and I'll head downstairs.

11. *Review yearbook outline for vetting with Ms. Bartel*
12. *Audrey: debating tournament?*

The thought of trying to talk to Audrey after making such an idiot of myself on Friday makes me nervous enough to want to write a list about things that make me nervous.

I glance at the clock. I have one more minute. I'll make this one quick.

I take another sheet of paper.

Things That Make Me Nervous
1. *People who drive too fast*
2. *Asking hot girls out (especially after I've made them run away)*
3. *Forgetting something important*

My fingers fly across the page, capturing words almost as quickly as I can think them.

4. *Shots at the nurse's office*
5. *The first time I tell someone I'm Jewish*
6. *Talking with Dad*

7. *Anything with Dad*

8. *Sweating when I start to feel panicky*

"Chick?" Mom's voice calls up to me.

I yell loudly so she can hear me through the door. "Yeah, Mom! I'm coming. I'll be down in, like, thirty seconds."

"Okay, honey."

I write faster.

9. *Talking with Audrey*

10. *The two hours before a test or exam*

11. *Swimming in the ocean*

I tap my pen against my teeth. One more, to make it a nice round dozen. I skim back over my list. Oh yeah. How about the most important one?

12. *Needing to make lists to keep my anxiety under control*

I realize that really that's thirteen, not twelve. Maybe I should split them up?

"Tadeusz!"

"Okay, okay!" It's a sign of impatience when Mom uses my full name. If she pulls out the *Yosef*, I'm done for.

I fumble for the key that's magnetized to the underside of my desk. I unlock the bottom drawer and slide it open.

I drop in the lists and slide the drawer shut. I lock it and replace the key in its hiding spot.

I stretch, grin and crack my knuckles. My stress has vanished.

I feel *awesome*.

I actually skip across my room to go help Mom with lunch.

Chapter Five

"Put Froot Loops on the list." Elijah turns the page in his book and takes another bite of his peanut-butter-and-banana toast. He's reading *Diary of a Wimpy Kid* for the nine hundredth time.

I write *Froot Loops* on the list. This is a Sunday-morning ritual for the three of us. Elijah, Mom and I have breakfast, and while we eat, I write our shopping list for the week. Mom made this my job in first grade when Mrs. Hodgins told her I needed to practice my printing. The teacher suggested I be put in charge of writing our grocery lists, and Mom was happy to comply.

She'd probably have a fit if she knew how deeply I have since taken Mrs. Hodgins's advice. I make about twelve lists every day. Some days I make twenty.

"Erase that, Chick. I am not buying Froot Loops."

"Why, Mom?" Elijah says it like it's one word: Whymom?

"You boys have enough sugar in your diets already. You don't need to add to it with junky cereals."

Pretty much anything that's not 100 percent bran, oats or spelt counts as junky for my mother.

"Please? Just as a one-time treat?" Elijah's voice rises an octave.

"Breakfast is not a time for high-sugar foods," Mom says. "It's important that your body gets a balance of protein, fat and carbohydrates to start your day. Otherwise your brain doesn't work properly."

Mom is full of these explanations. Depending on the topic, she can lay a killer argument on you that's backed by research and "best practices." She spends a lot of time reading about how to raise healthy kids.

"But Mom, I hate oatmeal."

"I never said you had to eat only oatmeal," she counters. "There are plenty of healthy options in the cereal aisle." She turns to me. "Chick, just write *cereal* on the list, and then when we're at the store, I'll let you choose, Elijah, okay?"

"Whoop-de-doo," Elijah says under his breath. He takes a bite of toast and turns another page.

"You're not supposed to read at the table," I say.

Elijah's head snaps up. "Yes, I can read at the table."

"No, you can't." I love getting him riled up until his voice climbs to a squeak.

"Yes I can! Just not during family meals," he adds.

"Well, what do you think this is?" Mom asks.

Elijah points at me. "He's writing a list."

I shrug. "I always write our lists on Sunday mornings."

"And anyway, Dad's not here, so it's not a real family meal," Elijah finishes. He puts the last bite of toast into his mouth.

He's got a point. I guess we're not technically complete without Dad. Although, come to think of it, Dad doesn't add much. Just stress.

"Can you please write ground flaxseed and quinoa too?" Mom says.

I groan. "When are you going to get off this health kick, Mom?"

She looks at me. "When have you ever known me not to be on a health kick?"

"Good point." It's pretty much a steady rotation of kale and lima beans around here.

She stacks our cereal bowls and puts them in the sink. "Chick, did you take your vitamins?"

"Yes."

"What about you, Elijah? Did you take your omegas? You need omegas for your brain, honey."

"My brain is good, Mom," Elijah says.

"I'm not saying your brain isn't good, Elijah. I'm saying omega-3 fatty acids are essential for helping your neurons work their best."

"You should have been a nutritionist, Mom," Elijah says.

"Totally," I say. "Forget the drop-in center. You should go work at Planet Organic."

Mom turns to flick me with the corner of her dishtowel. I pull away with a little scream of terror. Elijah laughs.

Dad appears at the kitchen doorway. Immediately, the air in the room changes. Mom folds the dishtowel and hangs it neatly on the stove handle. Elijah stops laughing and goes back to his book. I duck my head down and pretend to be writing, ignoring the way my underarms just broke out in sweat.

Dad crosses the kitchen and opens the cupboard above the phone. He takes an energy bar from the box in there. Breakfast for his golf game, I guess.

Elijah looks up. "Are we still going to get that poster paper later, Dad?" Elijah asks.

"What poster paper is that?"

Elijah has bugged him about this three times in the past week.

Why does Dad always make us explain ourselves, over and over again? He can't possibly have forgotten. It's like it's some sort of power play.

"For my natural-resources project," Elijah says.

"Can't you guys pick that up today?" Dad looks at Mom, who has suddenly become determined to get the coffee machine really, really clean.

"Sure we can," she says. "We can stop at the stationary store."

I write *poster paper* on the list. A bit of pressure eases.

"Dad, you said you'd take me today." Elijah sulks.

Dad sighs. "I won't be home until after two, and then I've got some paperwork I need to catch up on. Maybe before supper. If I have a chance. If you aren't able to pick some up first." He looks sideways at Mom.

Elijah sighs, longer and heavier. "Fine."

I wonder what it would feel like to be ignored and forgotten by Dad. Instead of being constantly under the microscope. The way he treats us is so different. I really got the shaft when God decided I'd go first. For some reason, all of Dad's unfulfilled dreams are pinned squarely on me as the firstborn child.

Well, at least one unfulfilled dream—I'm the one who has to go to law school since Dad never got a chance to. (Oh, and that's my fault too, since my unexpected arrival was the reason he had to quit pre-law and get a job at the bank. Even as an unborn fetus I was causing him headaches.)

I get scrutinized and criticized. Elijah barely gets noticed. It's bizarre.

I was hoping Dad would leave after getting his energy bar and hassling Elijah, but no such luck. He looks at me.

Mom sees it and tries to save me. "Bread and cheese, Chick. And garlic."

I write them down. Slowly. My fingers roll the pen between their tips, itching to write more. My pulse pounds as I wait for Dad to leave, but even as he's standing there, I'm making a list in my head. How will I fall short of his standards today? What will I forget to do?

"And what are you working on this afternoon, Tadeusz?"

As far back as I can remember, Dad has never called me Chick. Not once.

"A report," I say, but it comes out as a whisper. I clear my throat, but that only seems to make it narrower. "A report. For Social Studies. On the formation of political parties."

"When is it due?"

Crap. This is one detail I've missed.

My head spins. When did Mr. Gomez say the report was due? I swear I knew this when I looked at the assignment sheet last night.

"I'm not sure," I say. "Not for a week or so."

Dad takes a step closer and leans his hands on the breakfast bar. "In order to be successful in this life, you must always know what is expected of you. How are you supposed to manage your time if you don't even know when the report is due?"

I speak too quickly, which makes my words run together into a jumble. Dad looks at me like I'm some confused animal that's wandered out of the forest and vomited at his feet.

I back up and repeat myself. "The deadline is written on the assignment sheet. I have it upstairs." My heart is pounding so fast and hard that it's difficult for me to hear my own voice.

He grunts and his gaze slides away. He chooses a banana from the fruit bowl and leaves without another word to any of us.

Relief fills me. Still, my heart rate is high now, and I'm breathing in short little bursts. The three of us pretend not to listen as he puts on his jacket and shoes.

When the door to the garage closes behind him, Elijah speaks. "He's so unfair."

Mom sighs. "He's not trying to be unfair, honey. He's just busy and stressed out."

"Well, you're busy too, Mom," Elijah points out. He pushes his chair back from the table. "And you have a stressful job. But you're not mean."

I let my breath out very slowly.

1. Gas station?

"I don't have deadlines like your father does," Mom says. "Deadlines add a lot of pressure." She closes the fridge. "Can you write *potting soil*?"

I do.

"Maybe Dad needs to change jobs," Elijah grumbles. He starts toward the stairs.

And walk away from all that money? Like that would ever happen. He brought in nearly three million dollars in commissions last year on his own. I overheard him telling Uncle Cecil. Why would he quit that? Making money is the only thing that seems to make him happy.

I tap the pen against the tabletop, trying to turn my thoughts away from obsessing about making a list. Because making lists offsets the stress of thinking about how much I disappoint my dad.

But it's useless.

1. *Garden center (potting soil)*
2. *Library?*

"That's enough, Elijah," Mom says. Her voice says the subject is closed. "Now both of you, go get ready. We're leaving in twenty minutes."

I glance down at the shopping list, at my tidy printing and neatly numbered list items. I feel better. But I don't know how long it'll last.

Chapter Six

I go up to my room and change out of my pajama bottoms. Then I sit at my desk. I'll whip off a couple while I'm waiting for Mom to get ready.

Mom thinks I'm totally dedicated to my schoolwork. For her it's the best thing ever. She tells people that I'm a keener. "He comes right home from school and goes straight to his room to start his homework," she says.

If only she knew.

It's sad, actually. Most people my age hang out at friends' houses playing games or shooting hoops while I'm hunched over my desk, trying to keep my brain from flying apart.

Sometimes—like Friday, with Audrey—I even have to stop in the middle of what I'm doing to make a list. So I can get my composure back. Because if I reach a certain point of stress...I can't.

I'm not sure when I first began keeping lists. It's been a while now. A few years, maybe. It became a habit when I realized it calmed me down. And like habits seem to do, over time it has turned into something I *need*. The thought of trying to stop now makes me feel afraid. I don't think I could do it.

I glance at the deep drawer in my desk where I keep my lists. There must be thousands by now. Tens of thousands? I should chuck them. But that idea makes me feel queasy. There's something about knowing they're all here, in my drawer, that gives me some peace. They're like a security blanket.

The really funny thing? I never read them over. Once they're written, I can relax. Their purpose has been served, and I don't need them anymore. But I still can't throw them away.

I know this isn't normal. I've spent some time reading up on obsessive-compulsive disorder. When people hear the term OCD, they think about people who are always washing their hands or having to check and recheck that they locked the door or turned off the oven. Over and over.

But there's more than hand washing. There are all kinds of things people do to make themselves feel better. To make their obsessions go away. Some people count or do something a specific number of times to make sure they end on the right number. Some people pray or think good thoughts every time a bad thought happens, so they can "cancel" the bad thought out. Some people rearrange their sock drawers over and over.

I make lists.

We're unlocking a shopping cart when I see her across the parking lot. She's standing at the front entrance of the store.

She's dressed in her field-hockey uniform. White shirt, blue skirt, knee socks.

My stomach does a low dive as we start toward the entrance. I'm thrilled and terrified at the same time. My heart starts to beat faster.

She's standing behind a table piled high with white, red and green boxes. Krispy Kreme donuts. A fundraiser for her team.

She's alone. A couple of her teammates are at the other door, where people exit the store.

I want to run. And at the same time, I want to grab her and kiss her madly and smother her with my burning love.

I stare at her perfection as we walk toward the

entrance. I am helpless to look away. She hasn't noticed me yet.

What if she blows me off?

I fix my gaze on her neck where her hair pulls up into her ponytail. I could eat it.

Elijah rolls the cart up the curb. Audrey looks up as the automatic doors slide open. Elijah keeps rolling, straight through the doors and into the store entrance. Mom follows right behind, and then they're gone. It's a miracle.

Audrey sees me staring at her and smiles. She has the most incredible smile. It starts off slow, but then it spreads and lights up her entire face.

I think my heart will explode. I am acutely aware of the expression on my face. I am certain I look like one of those cartoon characters, all cross-eyed with little hearts floating above my head.

"Hi, Chick," she says.

"Hi," I breathe. Nothing else comes to mind.

A couple beats pass.

"Oh, listen," says Audrey. "I'm so sorry I took off the other day. Ms. Jeffs wanted to speak with me about the fundraiser, and I had to leave."

"Oh," I say. "That's okay." I suppose I should feel relieved that she hasn't figured out I'm a total freak, but I'm too distracted by her magnificence.

"So...you're shopping?" Audrey says.

"Yes. Yeah. Yup."

I nod, just in case she didn't get the message the first three times. I realize I'm being an idiot, but I seem helpless to behave otherwise.

"That's good."

There's another pause, and I realize I'm supposed to fill it.

"So...you're doing fundraising?" I point to the boxes on her table.

"Yeah, we are," she says. "It's going pretty well. I think the people on the other door are selling a lot more than me though."

I nod again. My mind flies around like a gnat in

a windstorm, desperate to land somewhere. I don't want our conversation to end, but I don't know what else to talk about.

"Are you going to buy a box?" Audrey asks.

"A box?"

She points to the donuts.

"Ah, oh. Well, ah, yes. We might," I say. "On our way out. I will. I'll make sure my mom buys some. For sure. I'll come back here and buy them from your table, so you can say you sold some donuts too. Not just the people at the exit."

I sound like I've got a talking disorder. My palms break out in sweat.

"Okay, cool." Audrey nods again and smiles. "So... what are you shopping for?"

I realize that she doesn't know what to say to me either. It gives me a boost of confidence. Which might be why I blurt out the next thing.

"Do you want to get together sometime so we can prepare for the tournament?"

Audrey's eyebrows go up.

Suddenly I wish I hadn't said anything. Maybe I wasn't reading her right. Maybe she was only being nice the other day because she thinks I'm a total doofus.

I open my mouth to tell her never mind, it was just a random suggestion. But before I can say anything, she says, "Sure. I'd love to."

It's my turn to look surprised.

I blink. "Uh. Okay. Great!" The tournament is two weeks away. What do I do now?

My head feels light. Oh. Crap. Next comes the— yup. There it is, my heart roaring out of the gates, hammering like a tin roof in a rainstorm. The nerves in my hands leap to attention, instantly craving the feel of a pen and paper.

"Do you want to call me sometime?" Audrey says, her voice muffled by the growing static in my head. "And then we can figure out when to meet and stuff."

"Sure," I bark. "Yes. Can I have your phone number?"

Oh God, please save me from myself.

"I'll write it down for you," Audrey says. She looks around on the table, but I spot the pen first. I slap my hand over it and pull a small square of paper toward me. A raffle ticket. "Is this okay to use?"

"Sure."

I flip it over and write her name on the back. "Okay, shoot." With a pen in my hand, my head clears a little and my breathing slows. I write the numbers as she says them, then *Audrey Hervieu*.

"Hey, you spelled it right!" she exclaims.

She watches as I keep writing.

"Your printing is so neat," she says. "It's, like, these perfect tiny little capital letters."

I snatch another little piece of paper. *Audrey thinks Chick's printing is cool*, I write.

She laughs again.

I do a smiley face, then straighten. I've got a big

silly grin of my own. But that's okay—she's wearing one too.

I fold up her number and fumble it into my pocket with sweaty fingertips. I push my dorky message across the table toward her.

I stare at her hands as she picks it up. Her nails are perfect. Clean. Short. Not fussy.

"Well, call me, then," Audrey says.

"You got it." I hold out the pen. Her fingers brush mine as she takes it. I almost fall over.

Somehow I find a few more words inside my head. "Good luck with the fundraiser."

"Thanks, Chick."

I spend the whole ride home twitching.

Nervous questions stack up in my mind, one on top of the other. About spending time alone with Audrey. About getting ready for the debating tournament.

I can't wait to get home so I can write them all down.

My hands burn. I ignore Mom and Elijah and instead try to distract myself with a graphic novel about clones. I try to breathe. I try to calm myself, to talk myself down from the growing panic inside me. Panic that if I can't write stuff down, I'm going to lose control.

But it doesn't work. There's only one thing that does.

Chapter Seven

My mood is edgy, to say the least, as I push a stack of chairs along the gym floor. I just want to get home and make a couple of lists, and then maybe chill out and listen to music for a while, but I have to set up five rows for tonight's band performance first. How come I always get stuck doing this kind of stuff? Sometimes it's a pain in the butt to have your teachers like you. And where is Finnian? He was supposed to be here ten minutes ago. And who cares about band anyway? There are better ways to spend a Monday night than sitting in a gym, listening to a bunch of hopeless nerds play hopelessly bad music.

Wait. What does that say about Debate Club?

I peel off my hoodie and glance at the clock. 3:27. It has been another monster-stress day. Mr. Gomez asked me to run for student council in the spring. Great. Another thing to pile onto my plate. Another thing to have Dad breathing down my neck about.

I wipe my sweating palms on my pants. Maybe I should try using antiperspirant on them. But what if I accidentally forgot I was wearing it and left big white streaks across the front of my thighs?

The thought makes me want to make a list of all the ways sweat is embarrassing.

When I've got all the chairs in rows, I move the music stand into place at the front and look up.

My heart stops. Maryke and Audrey are standing outside the gym doors. As I watch, Audrey pokes her head around the open door and looks at the band setup. She sees me and smiles.

I swallow. And sweat.

I don't think I can handle talking to her. I'll end up being rude to her. I can't control it. I need my fix, to get rid of the day's stress, before I can be normal again.

It's not you, it's me, I think.

I bite back a sudden giggle.

I have to get out of here. I can't talk to Audrey like this.

Just then the universe intervenes. Someone behind Audrey says something, and she turns to look.

And so I bolt, racing toward the double doors that lead outside. I smash through them without a backward glance.

Once outside, I don't stop running. I burn around the side of the building and hammer for the bushes that line the school property.

Id-i-ot. Id-i-ot.

My feet pound out the word, one-two-three, one-two-three, over and over as I pelt toward home. I run the whole way, all seven blocks. Soccer lungs.

I take the front steps in a single leap, turning my shoulder sideways and smashing it against the door to break my speed. This would be a very bad time for the neighbors to be looking out their windows.

With shaking hands, I crush my key into the lock and slam the door open.

I scrape one shoe off but only get my foot half out of the other one. Doesn't matter. I keep moving, taking the stairs two at a time.

The toe of my sneaker catches on the top of the stairs, and I go sprawling. I grunt as my chest hits the floor. My palms squeal as they burn across the hardwood. One fist slams into the hallway table and a vase of flowers rolls off the top, thunking to the floor and soaking me in a slosh of water and petals. The bottom of the heavy vase leaves a dent in the hardwood floor. Mom's going to love that.

I get my feet under me and stagger toward my room, a gorilla in an earthquake. The cold metal of the doorknob slides around inside my sweaty grip.

And then I'm in.

My hands stretch ahead of me, reaching as I run for my desk. I snatch at the paper stack with two hands, sending a spray of loose paper into the corner.

Pen. Pen. Pen.

My lips shape the word as my right hand dives for the jar. Too fast. I overshoot, plowing my fingers into the side of the container. It leaps off the desk. The pens hit the floor, fanning out everywhere.

I moan.

I leap into the middle of the pen spray and snatch up a blue one. I crouch on the rug, smoothing out the paper that my sweating hand has crumpled. I yank the cap off the pen with my teeth and spit it across the room. My fingers slip on the shaft of the pen, and the nib punches through the paper. I can't write on the carpet. Groaning, I crawl a couple of yards to the hardwood.

I pull the first thing out of my brain.

How to Know There's Something Really Wrong with You

1. Go to school
2. Act normal
3. Pretend you're interested in other people's conversations when really, all you can think about is making a stupid LIST
4. Fight the urge, every minute of the day, to write a stupid LIST

With each number, my messy scrawl becomes larger and angrier. My heart is pounding in my throat. My ears ring.

5. Fake smile and laugh while dying to escape
6. Be a grumpy, surly jerk because you need to

get away from school so bad (because you
need to get home and make a stupid LIST)

7. Take off on your new girlfriend because you
    can't handle being nice to her because you
    have to MAKE A STUPID LIST

8. Run home like a big stupid fricking BABY

A sob escapes me as I write this last one.

My mind flashes back to the flowers lying on the
floor.

9. Destroy stuff in your desperation to make
    your stupid LIST

10. Cry like a big stupid fricking BABY because
    you realize there's something really stupidly
    wrong with you that you need to act this way

By number ten I'm still breathing hard, but my
heart rate has returned to something less like a
freight train. I stop writing and sit back on my heels.

I look at the scattered pens and paper that surround me. What a mess.

I wipe my face with my hands.

I leave everything where it is and go out into the hallway. I pick up the vase. I put new water in it. I replace any flowers that are still in one piece and put the broken ones in my bathroom garbage. I take a hand towel and mop up the water from the floor, running my fingers over the dent in the hardwood. I hope Mom doesn't notice it.

I wipe the splashes off the wall, then go back into my bedroom. I close the door behind me and survey the disaster.

I cross the rug to my desk and unlock the drawer of endless lists. I pull a bunch out and flip through them. The one I recently wrote about Audrey is on the top.

I scan the titles. *Points to Remember in a Debate. Elijah's Irritating Table Manners. Places My Father Goes to Avoid His Family. How to Look Busy So Mom*

Doesn't Make Me Do Chores. Persuasive Speaking Skills. Why Cynical People Suck. Occasions Where Finnian's Loud Farts Have Made People Laugh. Mom's Epic Recipe Fails. My Favorite Memories from When I Was Little.

I don't even remember making some of these.

I drop the bundle of lists onto my desk. I feel suddenly exhausted.

I gather up the blank sheets of paper that are strewn around the floor. I replace them neatly on the pile on my desk. I stoop to pick up the pen jar, then drop to my knees. I crawl around the rug, gathering pens and putting them back into the jar. My hands are shaking.

This is so messed up.

I catch a glimpse of myself in the full-length mirror. I feel a shock to see the crouching, wild-haired, tear-streaked goblin reflected back at me.

I put my head down on the floor and cry.

Chapter Eight

I hear the garage door opening as I'm getting into the shower. Mom's home.

I don't want to think about what might have happened if she had returned ten minutes earlier. And what if Elijah had been here?

What if Dad had come home?

As I step under the warm stream, an involuntary shudder shakes me. I feel a sudden urge to puke.

I take a big mouthful of water. I gargle, then spit.
I take another one. I swish the water around in my
mouth. Spit.

Whatever happens, Dad can never know about
this. He would freak out if he knew his kid had
something wrong with him.

Something even more wrong, I mean. I already
know he thinks I'm not smart enough or strong
enough or organized enough. If he knew about the
lists, he would think I'm crazy too.

I scrub my face.

Am I crazy?

How do I get away from this? *How do I stop?*

In frustration, I turn the shower handle all the
way to *Cold*. The water shocks my skin and I gasp.
I want to pull away, but I force myself to stay under
the frigid spray for a few seconds.

I look at the letters on the tap. *Cold*. I rearrange a
few and drop another.

OCD.

When I can't stand it any longer, I turn the handle back to the warm setting. I take a deep breath and splash more water on my face. I feel much better.

I squeeze a little blob of shampoo into my palm and rub my hands together. A manly, woodsy smell fills the shower. I soap up my hair. Mom calls to me, but I ignore it. If she needs to tell me something badly enough, she'll come stand outside my bathroom door.

I feel kind of calm after my impulsive arctic bath. It's like I shocked myself back into a normal state. I wonder if I could do something at school to pull myself out of the anxiety zone when it starts to get heavy. Could I pinch myself or something? Or maybe find a way to deliver an electric shock?

Yeah, that would go over well—a teacher discovering I was carrying around a tiny electric cattle prod. They'd send me to a shrink faster than you can say *aberrant sensation seeking*.

And if that ever got back to my dad...

I rinse the bubbles out of my hair and stand under the water for a few more minutes, until my goose bumps are gone.

I step out onto the warm tiles and reach for a towel. I hit a switch and the fan whirs to life.

I use the towel to rub a circle on the mirror so I can see my reflection. I lean close, inspecting my chin for any possible whisker growth. Last year Garrett Blume told me that if you just start shaving, your hair grows in faster. But I don't think it's working. I've shaved my entire beard area three times in the last month, and all that keeps growing back are these little fuzzy blond hairs.

I scan my groin. Nope. Nothing there either.

I finish toweling off. My stomach grumbles as I climb back into my jeans. Maybe I'll go help Mom get supper ready.

I whistle as I run the towel around on the

floor with my foot, mopping up the drips. I throw the towel into the laundry hamper and open the bathroom door.

The first thing I see is Audrey. She's standing on the other side of the room. Near my desk.

The second thing I see is the look of surprise on her face.

The third thing I see is the bundle of papers she's holding in her hands.

Chapter Nine

What are you doing here? My brain asks the question, but my lips don't move.

Why didn't I put everything away and lock the drawer? When do I *ever* forget to do that?

If this is a joke that God is playing on me, then He got me good.

Audrey and I stare at each other for a long time.

Then she sets the papers down on my desk. She swallows. "I'm sorry," she says.

Sorry for what? For not knowing she was getting involved with a schizo crazypants? For even talking to me in the first place?

"How did you get in here?" I ask. My level voice surprises me.

"Your mom."

Mom never just lets people go upstairs. She must be super happy about Audrey coming over to bend her own rules like that.

I can't think of anything to say. I wait for the head rush to begin, but it doesn't. I am strangely calm.

Audrey glances down at the stack of lists. She looks back at me. "I'm sorry," she says again. "I think I should leave."

I stand, paralyzed and speechless, and watch her go.

For the next week during Debate Club, it's like nothing ever happened. We still talk and take notes and nod when Mr. Chadderton gives us tips. But we're not *talking* talking.

It's Friday by the time I summon enough courage to approach Audrey. I have so many things to say. *I'm sorry* being chief among them. I don't know what she thinks about me, but I do know she saw the list about her, because it was in the pile she was holding. And even though *she* was in *my* room, looking at *my* things, I have this need to apologize. And to find out if she thinks I'm a total freak.

The thought of talking to her makes me sweat. I focus on breathing deeply, so that when I round a corner and find her standing at her locker, I don't faint from stress.

"Audrey."

She turns. When she sees it's me, she turns

back to her locker. But she's standing in a way that doesn't shut me out entirely. So I go closer, until I'm standing next to her. I cut straight to the chase.

"Did you read the list about you?"

Audrey blushes, and I know she found it. I am so glad I didn't write anything about her boobs on that list. Because they're right up there with all the other stuff I like about her.

"I'm glad you like my fingernails," she says shortly.

I swallow. "I'm really sorry."

"You have nothing to be sorry for."

"I do."

She sighs then, and shakes her head. "No. I was in your private space." She looks down. "It's snoopy to read someone else's stuff."

"Pretty hard to resist."

She smiles a little, and I breathe again. Then I

take a huge chance. "That list isn't finished yet. I still have more to add."

"Oh." She tucks her hair behind her ear. I love the way she does it. I want to ask her to marry me, to bear all my children, to live on a mountainside farm with me and grow roses and rainbows.

She smiles a little and looks at me then. "I...only came to your house because I wanted to give you my number. You dropped it the other day when you went into the store. And then when I tracked you down in the gym on Monday, you left before I could catch you."

My mind flashes back to my bionic rush home the other afternoon. What must she think of me?

"I didn't mean to be rude on Monday," I say. "I just had to get home."

"Were you avoiding me?"

"Not at all," I lie.

"Why did you run off then?"

I pause, looking at Audrey's face for a long minute. "Did you read the list called *How to Know There's Something Wrong With You?*"

"I think so. Is that the one about making lists?"

"There's your explanation."

She's quiet for a moment. But when she speaks, it's with curiosity, not *wow-buddy-you're-really-weird*-ness. "Why do you make so many?"

I sigh. Where do I start?

She shakes her head. "It's none of my business." She bends down and reorganizes the books inside her bag to make room for her pencil case. Her brown ponytail fans out across her back.

"No, it's…it's okay," I say. And it is okay. I feel relieved to finally talk to someone about it. "It's not your fault. I usually keep them locked up. That big drawer is full of them."

"I know," she says, straightening. "You left it open."

I did, too. Awesome. She must really think I'm a whack job.

I summon every molecule of courage that's available to me. "Can I walk with you?"

"Sure." We turn and start down the hallway. "I didn't read them all, you know," Audrey says. "I only saw the ones on the desk."

Oh. Good then. So she saw only, like, fifty of them. Great.

She smiles and looks at me in that way she has. "You take debating very seriously."

I laugh, but there's no humor in it. "I couldn't care less about debating," I say.

"Well. You're good at it." She smiles, and I melt a little.

"Thanks. So are you."

"Why are you in Debate Club if you couldn't care less about debating?" she says.

"I do it because my dad wants me to."

"Ah," says Audrey. "Well, what would you rather be doing?"

I shrug. "I like writing a lot better than debating."

She looks at me. "Is that why you make so many lists?"

I clear my throat. "Not really. Making lists is a stress-management thing," I say. "It helps me remember stuff. And it lets me feel like I have some control when things feel out of control."

"Like, stressful?"

I nod.

"Does your dad stress you out?"

"You could say that. I get stressed out about other things too. But I think he's at the root of it. I don't want to screw up and make him mad, you know? So I feel like I have to get everything right."

Audrey nods. "I get that. My dad doesn't stress me out, but sometimes other things feel pretty hard, you know?"

I breathe a little. Man, she's easy to talk to.

"When I feel like it's really over the top, I go for a run," she adds.

"That explains those legs of yours," I say.

She blushes. "As if. But that's my steam valve. Running."

"Well, listing is mine." I can't believe I said that so casually. Mind you, Audrey hasn't seen me in a panic. Like, truly *listing*.

I get an image of a ship tilting in heavy waves, trying to right itself. Huh. That's kind of perfect.

"I could think of worse ways to let off stress," Audrey says.

"Yeah...I'm not so sure," I say. "The urge to do it is pretty intense sometimes. Like, freaky intense."

I look at her face to see what her reaction is going to be. But she doesn't look like she's going to run away screaming. She's listening.

"Well, so, what's the big deal?" Audrey asks.

"What do you mean?"

"Like...so what if you make lists?" She shrugs.

I blink.

She shrugs again. "Who cares?" she says. "Everybody has their things, right? I go for a run.

Some people need to listen to music. Some people meditate."

"Um, yeah, but you don't need to run, like, ten times a day. Have you heard the term *obsessive-compulsive disorder*?"

"Yeah."

"Well, I'm a compulsive list maker."

"So?"

"What do you mean, so?"

"Well, it's not like you're washing your hands every five minutes or cleaning your desk with Clorox wipes or anything."

I shake my head. "It's not normal."

She throws her head back and laughs. "That is the dumbest thing I've ever heard you say, Chick."

"What?"

"Who even knows what normal is? There is no such thing as *normal*." She gives me a little shove.

"You don't think it's weird?"

"Of course it's weird. We're all weird."

"You're not weird."

She raises an eyebrow. "You don't know me very well."

"Yet," I say. I smile.

She smiles back. "Yet."

Chapter Ten

Audrey and I agree to meet after school on Tuesday. Debate prep and all.

By the time the bell goes at the end of art class, I'm out the door. I hurry around the corner of the strip mall to the DQ. I settle myself at a table. I should have a few minutes before she arrives.

I pull out my math notebook and flip to the blank pages at the back.

Things I Want to Know about Audrey

1. *Do you twirl your hair in class because you're self-conscious or because you're bored? Or because you know it looks cute?*

2. *Do you really like hanging out with Shazia and Maryke? Do they talk about anything else but manga and Liam Hemsworth?*

3. *Why do you say you're weird?*

I peer around, but there's no one else here but me. I'll be able to scribble a few things quickly before anyone else shows up for their after-school junkfest. And besides, Audrey already knows about my addiction. Obsession. Compulsion.

My chest loosens a little.

4. *Have you ever stuffed your bra?*

5. *What's it like to share a room with your little sister?*

6. *What's the worst supper you've ever made?*

I tap my pen on my teeth. We walked to my house last Friday with the idea of working on our arguments for the debate, but mostly we ended up talking. For two hours. Mom invited her to stay for dinner, but Audrey said she had to get home to make dinner for her dad and sister.

7. *Where did your mom go? And why hasn't she ever been in touch? Does it hurt?*
8. *What is your favorite food?*
9. *Have you ever been kissed?*
10. *Do you think about us naked?*

I scribble this last one out and replace it with:

10. *What part of your body do you like the most?*

I'd better stop thinking about Audrey's naked body. And anyway, this list is finished. Ten is a nice round number.

I flip the page and start a new one.

Career Ideas That Interest Me

1. *Author/illustrator: work from home*
2. *Coast Guard: six weeks on, six weeks off*
3. *Pro soccer: duh!*
4. *Game writer: playing games and writing stories all day*
5. *Geneticist: solving major diseases*

"Hey."

I jump and slam my notebook shut. "Jesus."

"Whoa! Sorry. I didn't mean to scare you." Audrey smiles and tucks her hair behind her ear. "I thought you would hear me coming."

My heart is going a mile a minute. "I guess I was absorbed."

"I didn't think Jewish people believed in Jesus."

"We don't. Well, we do. We just don't think he's the messiah."

Audrey sits down across from me. "What's a messiah?"

"A messenger. Why are you asking me about Jesus?"

"Because you said *Jesus* when I startled you." She takes off her jacket.

"Oh. Yeah, I guess I shouldn't."

She shrugs and smiles. "Doesn't bother me. I've never met the guy." She nods at my book. "Can I see?"

I hesitate. "You can see this one," I say, opening to the page with the career list and sliding it across the table. "Not the one on the page before."

"Ooh, is there something nasty on that page?" Audrey fakes like she's going to flip the page. I slap her hand down onto the table, pinning it there.

"Okay, I won't." She laughs. "I promise."

My stomach seesaws as she looks into my eyes. I leave my hand where it is, covering hers. She doesn't pull away.

She holds my gaze for a moment, and then she pulls the book toward her with her other hand. She looks at the list.

"Coast Guard," she says. "Nice." She reads farther. "Pro soccer. Would that fly with your dad?"

I snort. "None of these would fly with my dad. He only wants me to be a lawyer." Dad lives in daily regret that he missed that boat. But now—hurrah!—he's got me to sail it.

"Not even a geneticist? That takes a medical degree and everything. And game writers can make, like, more than a hundred grand."

I turn Audrey's hand over and lace my fingers with hers. My brain goes all floaty, but in a good way. "Nope. It's lawyer or bust."

"Pfft. I'd say bust then, if it was me," she says. She squeezes my hand, and my heart does a somersault. "Is that why he's so into you being on the debate team?"

I nod. "Preparation for the real world." I echo the words he's said to me so many times. I change the subject. "What can I get you?" I nod toward the menu board.

Audrey looks over at the menu. A bored DQ employee snaps her gum and stares out the front door.

She turns back to me. "Skor Blizzard," she says. "Kid size."

"Kid size?"

She shrugs. "Have to watch my legs." Then she winks.

"As if," I say. I reach under the table and squeeze her thigh. She squeals. And then she looks at me in that way she has.

I might die of cute overload.

But instead, I stand. "One Skor Blizzard coming right up."

I order her a medium. And a banana split for myself.

"Have you ever stood up to him?" she asks when I bring our food to the table.

"Who, Jesus?"

Audrey laughs. I love the sound of it. She's so small, but her laugh is this huge throaty thing.

"No," she says, then laughs some more. "No, silly. I mean your dad."

I like how she calls me silly.

"What, like told him no?" I take a scoop of hot-fudge-covered soft-serve. "That's not an option with my old man."

"Or just tell him what you want to do," Audrey says. "You don't necessarily have to say no to what he wants. But you could tell him what you want. You know. Put it out there."

I watch as she spoons a bit of ice cream into her mouth. I could watch her eat all day.

I shake my head. "You can't do that with my dad. He's not what you'd call flexible."

"My way or the highway?"

"Something like that."

Audrey turns her spoon around and licks the back.

That is one lucky piece of plastic.

"What about your mom?" she asks.

"What, tell her I don't want to do what Dad wants me to do?" I ask. "She already knows that. It won't make any difference."

Audrey looks at me. "Does your mom do everything your dad says too?"

I think about that. "I don't know," I say finally. "I never see them talk. Unless it's about me or my brother. They never just hang out."

"That's sad."

"It is kind of sad," I agree. Mom is always so alive when Dad isn't around. But as soon as he shows up, she turns into this quiet ghost who doesn't say anything. It's like he sucks the life force out of her.

"You should stand up to him," Audrey says.

She makes it sound so simple. Like it's something I could *do*.

I shake my head. "I don't think so. He makes my life miserable enough, thanks. I don't need to add to it."

"Maybe he needs someone to stand up to him. I think sometimes people like that don't realize they're bullies until someone points it out to them."

"I don't think standing up to my dad will make him change his ways."

She shrugs and licks her spoon clean. "You'll never know unless you try it."

"I think this is one of those things you can predict without actually having to try it."

"You have no evidence to base your assertion on," she says. "It's all conjecture."

"Now you're pulling out the debate speak," I say. "I should know better than to try and argue with you."

"You should. I will argue you into the floor."

"That's why you're my partner." I grin. "You leave no stone unturned."

She looks at me. "Neither should you. Never concede defeat before you've even raised your sword."

"Is this a challenge?"

"It is now." Audrey leans forward and snatches a spoonful of my whipped cream.

"Hey!" I bat her spoon out of the way. Whipped cream splatters onto the table.

"Oh, now it's getting messy," Audrey says. She dives for more of my banana split.

"You're going down," I say, stabbing my spoon into her Blizzard.

"No way!" she shrieks, then giggles wildly.

It takes us a while to finish our ice cream, and we don't end up doing much debate prep after all.

As I walk Audrey home, I can feel my anxiety cranking up. The pressure is building. I should be enjoying my first real date with my first real girlfriend. But all I can think about is how stressed out I feel at the thought of standing up to my dad.

And all I can hear is Audrey's voice saying, *Never concede defeat before you've even raised your sword.*

Chapter Eleven

That evening seems as good a time as any to give it a shot.

I launch my first missile as the salad bowl makes its rounds. "So I'm thinking about my options for next term," I say, scraping a pile of spinach and green onion onto my plate.

Mom holds out the little bowl of nutritional yeast.

Hippie dust, my uncle calls it. "Take some, Chick," she urges. "It's good for your vitamin B12."

I dutifully take a spoonful and sprinkle it on my salad.

"And folate. And protein," Elijah adds. "You need it for your brain, you know." He speaks in an exaggerated New York accent that apes our Brooklyn roots.

I smirk.

Mom shoots him a look and passes the bowl in his direction. "You too, Mr. Wise Guy."

This makes Elijah laugh. "Mom. You're perfect."

Mom turns her attention to me. "What do you mean, options?" she says. "You don't start those until tenth grade."

"Mom, this is Chick we're talking about. He holds the record for Most Anal Kid Ever to Live," says Elijah. "He needs to plan ahead. Eighth grade is not a moment too soon."

"I'm not talking about classes," I say, ignoring him. "I'm talking about clubs." I pour dressing over my salad. "They fill up fast, and you can't always get the ones you want." So far, my dad has remained stony silent at his end of the table. Nothing new there.

"I always get the ones *I* want," says Elijah.

"Well, Introductory Butt Wiping and Whining For Dummies don't exactly have a lot of competition," I say.

Elijah boots me under the table. "Fart eater."

I snort. "They have a club for that too. They've specifically asked you to join."

"Boys!"

But I've cracked Elijah up, and he's not mad anymore.

Dad picks this time to enter the conversation. "I can't imagine Debate Club being so full that you can't get in." He hasn't touched his fork yet.

And just like that, my brain tightens up and I can't get enough air.

"I might like to try something different," I venture.

"Such as?"

Elijah looks at me, interested in hearing how I'm going to handle this one. He knows better than to get involved when Dad's talking to me.

An uncomfortable silence follows Dad's question.

Mom leans forward and picks up the bowl of roasted vegetables. "Elijah, honey, take another scoop." Her voice is a shade higher than normal.

Her attempt to deflect the tension doesn't distract Dad. He's sitting taut as a pointer dog, eyes focused on me with laser-like precision.

"Maybe screenwriting or game design," I say.

Dad stares. "Screenwriting?"

How is it that the quieter he speaks, the more nervous I feel?

Mom springs up from her end of the table. "Does anybody want more macaroni?"

Nobody answers. Mom is looking at Elijah. Elijah's looking at my dad. My dad is looking at me.

And I'm looking at my plate. The tops of my ears are burning. I force a deep breath into my lungs.

I can't possibly do this.

My brain feels all scrambled. The panic starts to rise.

I think about the jar of pens sitting on my desk. I could excuse myself and say I have to use the washroom.

And then I think about Audrey.

No. I can't give up. I have to tell him I'm quitting Debate Club after this term.

I take a deep breath and look up, straight into his face. I open my mouth. And what do I do?

I chicken out.

"It'll help me prepare better for my debates," I say. "Anticipating what the other speakers are going to say."

Dad looks at me for a moment, like maybe I'm something small and oddly jointed that flew through the open window. Then he grunts. He rearranges his forks with precision before picking one up. Breathing resumes around the table.

Crisis averted.

But I am no further ahead.

Eating, clearing and washing up takes forever, and I'm shaking with rage by the time I'm able to escape to my room. I sit down on the window bench.

I'm barely seated before my hand hits the page, blazing its angry trail of words. I don't stop until I've written down all the things I'm dying to say to my dad.

Later, I make doubly sure I've locked my drawer before I turn out the light.

Chapter Twelve

"I think we're done," Audrey says. "We've covered every possible angle." She's sitting on my sofa, her knees drawn up to her chest.

I glance at the clock. "Wow, it's already ten after eleven. Sure, let's call it a day. Or a night." I grin.

"How are things going with your dad?" she asked.

Earlier this evening I gave in to Audrey's pestering and showed her a few more lists. Including the one of the things I'm dying to say to my father. She made me read it out loud to her a few times. Then she told me I should give it to him.

I told her I would rather go parachuting without a backpack.

"Things are…you know." I shrug. "Same old, same old."

"Did you…?"

"Draw my sword and wade into battle?" I finish. "I gave it the old college try. He wasn't, ah, receptive, shall we say. He did come and try to talk to me later though." I tell her how he knocked on my door after supper.

"What did he say?"

I shrug. "I didn't answer."

"Why not?"

"It was too weird."

"I don't get it. Why is it weird that your dad knocked on your door?"

"You have to know, my dad never knocks on my

door. I don't even remember the last time he set foot in my room."

I don't remember the last time he asked to speak with me either. Usually, if Dad wants to talk, he just talks. He doesn't ask.

Audrey looks at me for a long time. "That sucks."

I shrug. "It is what it is. Well, I shouldn't say I ignored him. That wouldn't have gone over very well. I told him I had a test I had to study for and he went away."

"Maybe you should have let him in."

"Maybe."

As if.

The house is dark when I return from walking Audrey home.

I close the front door quietly and slide the deadbolt into place. I stand for a moment in the front hallway, listening. As if on cue, my tummy rumbles.

I head for the kitchen.

I flick on the little light above the stove and rummage for the cereal. I reach for a bowl and set it on the counter. Dad's phone pings, sending a flush of adrenaline into my belly.

Once my heart has slowed down, I pour milk on my cereal. I eat it standing up. My eyes rove the counter, looking for something to read. Dad's phone is sitting on top of a hardcover book. I move it to the side so I can see what he's reading. Usually he carries around magazines with no pictures, just pages and pages of complicated sentences. He's not much of a book reader.

The title of the book surprises me. *Listening with Love*? Weird. That's more of a Mom book than a Dad book, if you ask me.

I flip through the book as I eat. The feeling of weirdness grows. Why is my dad reading a book with chapter headings like "You Don't Always Have to Be Right," "Finding That Deeper Connection" and

"There Is Safety in Feeling Heard"?

Huh. I hope he reads that last one twice.

A little paper marks his place. I flip to it. It's a sticky note with his writing on it.

Glen Rosin. #3-1862 Virginia Avenue

Who is Glen Rosin? Is this his book? Maybe he's a client of my dad's.

I finish my cereal and rinse the bowl before putting it into the dishwasher. I clonk my toe on the drawer beneath the oven as I reach to turn the light out. Ow. Every. Bloody. Time.

I freeze, listening, but the noise doesn't wake anyone.

Once I'm upstairs, I punch Glen Rosin's name into my browser. I add "Virginia Avenue" to narrow the search.

Dr. Glen Rosin, clinical counselor.

Counselor? My dad's seeing a shrink?

Anger. Family of origin issues. Personal growth. Parent-child conflict.

I stare at my phone for a long time.

Either I've walked through a time warp and ended up in another life entirely...or my dad is trying to change.

Chapter Thirteen

I get up early on Saturday morning and force myself to eat breakfast. My stomach is a tangle of butterflies, but it's a different feeling from the usual anxiety. I think Audrey and I will flatten the opposition. I suspect Mr. Chadderton thinks so too.

Our school is sending six of us—three teams of two. It's not the biggest tournament ever, but there will be a dozen middle schools in total. The schools that win this tournament will go on to regionals in early spring. In high school, you can compete for nationals.

Which I'm sure Dad fully expects I will do.

After breakfast I head upstairs to get organized. I make one last list: tips for public speaking.

I shower and get dressed. I have to do my tie three times before I get the knot in the right place. My heart starts to patter a little too fast. I take a deep breath and hold it.

Mom calls up to me. "Are you ready, Chick?"

I release my breath in a quick whoosh. "Yeah, Mom!" I yell back.

My desk is still a mess after my meeting with Audrey last night. I find the debate file folder and stuff it into my courier bag. I double-check that my extra deodorant is in there too. One can never be too scentless.

I sling the bag over my shoulder and take the stairs two at a time.

Elijah is still asleep, his door closed. The lucky schmuck gets a whole morning with no one in the house to bother him.

My mother is standing at the bottom of the stairs, pink-cheeked and smiling. "Your dad's warming up the car," she says. "Are you excited? I'm so excited to watch you, honey."

"Mom, you've watched a debate before."

"I know, but this is your first tournament. It's an occasion!" She hugs me.

When she lets me go, I grin and smooth my shirt. "Let's go."

The drive to G.E. Wilkinson is long. I can feel Dad's eyes on me in the rearview mirror. I pretend to jot notes for the debate so I don't have to look up.

By the time we pull into a parking spot, the lot is already half full.

"I'm going to bolt," I say, gathering my bag. "I want to run something past Mr. Chadderton before we start."

"We'll look for you in there," Mom says. "Good luck, sweetie!"

Then my dad speaks. "Chick," he says. "Just a minute." He starts to unbuckle his seat belt.

But this is the last thing I can deal with today. "Sorry, Dad," I say. "I gotta blaze." There'll be hell to pay. But I can't let him rattle me.

I slam the door before I can hear his response.

I'm all the way across the parking lot when it hits me that he didn't call me Tadeusz.

He called me Chick.

"We're up last," says Audrey. She drops her binder onto the table and slips into the chair beside me. I move mine closer.

I open my folder and pull out a blank sheet from behind all the others. No one's going to think it's odd that I'm writing a list in the tense moments leading up to a debate. Iyengar is leafing through his notes, and Johnna is scribbling furiously.

I'll keep things on topic.

Effective Debating Strategies

1. *Straight, relaxed posture. Shoulders back*
2. *Projecting your voice from the diaphragm, not your chest*
3. *Eye contact with the judges*
4. *Strongest arguments first*

Mr. Chadderton pokes his head into our room. "Okay, everybody. The judges are set up."

My head starts to feel a little floaty. The others stand and push their chairs in. Should I try to look for Mom and Dad in the audience? Or is that a stupid idea?

"We're starting with Randy and Johnna, up against a team from Maria Montessori." Mr. Chadderton reads from a sheet of paper.

Audrey looks at me. "Do you want to go in and watch?"

"Maybe in a while."

She glances at my list, then at my face. She nods.

I breathe deeply as Johnna and Randy file through the doorway.

"Good luck, you guys," Audrey stage-whispers.

Randy gives her a thumbs-up.

Instinctively, I close the folder as Gary passes our table.

He holds out his hand. "Break a leg."

I slap his hand. "You guys too."

Iyengar fakes a sudden pain in his leg and limps out the door, moaning. Gary smothers a laugh.

The door closes behind Iyengar and Gary, and Audrey and I are left alone.

"You okay?" she asks.

"Not at all."

Concern knits her brow.

"Don't worry," I say. "I won't flake out on you or anything. We'll kick butt." I open my folder again. I wish I could believe the words I'm telling her. It's just that…my dad…and a debate. Both in the same building at the same time. Today is going to be one hellish day.

It's interesting that Audrey and I are debating the assertion that today's youth are overprogrammed. I don't consider myself overprogrammed. Debate Club and soccer are the only two things I do. But I'm supposed to do my two things like a boss. And I do. I was voted MVP of our soccer team at the end of last season. And I'm always the first person people turn to when they need help refining an argument. They talk to me even before they go to Mr. Chadderton. And usually my team comes out on top when the debates roll.

Still, it's not good enough. It's never good enough for him.

Audrey and I are arguing against the assertion. Persuading the judges that today's youth aren't overprogrammed. Even though people in my own class are under some serious pressure. People like Annie Allers, who does three different kinds of dance as well as violin. Or Devon Poon, who plays piano and has to go to Chinese school all day on Saturdays.

Sometimes I wonder what this does to your brain—having to persuade other people that you're right and they're wrong when you don't even believe what you're saying. How does that not mess up a person's mind?

I could never be a lawyer.

"I don't really care if we kick butt or not," Audrey says. She doesn't believe in our position either.

"Well, if we don't, I'll be disowned. So fake it."

She smiles.

I pick up my pen. "Give me three tips for conducting a good debate."

"Um, a loud voice."

"Already got that."

She reads over my list. "Speak with conviction. And take notes during the other team's rebuttal."

I write these down. My anxiety eases a little.

"Use hand gestures to engage your audience and strengthen your position."

"Good one," I say. I scratch the words onto the paper in front of me. "You forgot one."

"What?"

I put my pen down and take her hand. "Pick a wicked partner."

Audrey smiles. And then I kiss her.

Chapter Fourteen

As Audrey and I finish the first round of our debate, I can feel we've done well. Our preparation is paying off. The other team can feel it. So can the audience.

"We'll take a short break so the teams can prepare their rebuttals," says the debate host. The air in the room changes as the audience moves around, rustling and chatting.

I release a deep breath and take a sip of water to keep my nerves under control. I'm not feeling overly jittery. Maybe because I'm in my zone. Maybe because I'm still high after kissing Audrey.

Audrey and I huddle together at the table behind our podium, scanning each other's notes. Audrey will lead the rebuttal, and I'll deliver our closing arguments. And then we'll win the trophy and it'll all be over and I won't have to worry about it again for another five months.

"This is good," Audrey says, pointing at something I've scribbled in my notes. "I'm going to use this." She bends her head over the page as she writes. I wonder if she's still thinking about the kiss.

"You lead," I say.

"I know."

"I think we have this one."

"I know."

Even so, there's work to be done. Audrey has to nail our rebuttal, and I have to somehow link it back to our strongest argument. One badly constructed phrase, one moment of hesitation in the wrong place, could cost us the debate.

My stomach tightens.

No. I'm not going to think about that. Losing this debate is not a possibility I can consider.

The bell dings. We take our places behind the podium. The audience swims before me, a hundred or so faces turned in our direction. Waiting. Expectant.

I know my parents are out there somewhere. But I haven't looked for them. What I don't know won't hurt me.

"We now begin the final round," announces the debate host.

As the first guy on the other team, Boyd, begins his closing argument, my file folder slides off the podium. *Shffwwssshhhhh.*

It's a teeny-tiny cosmic joke on the day I least need it. The corner hits the hard floor of the stage—*thwack!*—and the folder smashes open, spraying my notes all over the place.

Mortified, I drop into a squat and quickly sweep my notes together. I have to crawl a little to reach a few of them. Those suckers can fly pretty far.

The other team doesn't stop, and for that I send a silent thank-you. Nobody onstage pauses or even acknowledges me. Audrey keeps her eyes on Boyd, providing me with a gracious cover. Smoothing over a big embarrassment, making it a minor incident.

I don't look at the audience, although I can guarantee that half of them are watching me instead of the debate.

I slide the last couple of sheets toward me, my fingers scrambling the pages back into the folder. It occurs to me that I could have just left everything where it was. It's not like I need my notes or anything. I already know my final argument inside and out.

Too late now.

I swallow my mortification and smooth my face into a look of total disinterest. I can't do anything about my wild blushing, but at least I can wear an expression that says this is no big deal.

I stand and place my folder back in its spot, being absolutely certain that it's well back from the lip of the podium this time, with no chance of falling off.

Boyd has finished his speech. I didn't hear a word of it.

Audrey clears her throat for our rebuttal. I should pay attention to this, because I'm supposed to be tying up all the loose ends in a couple minutes' time.

But my mind is anywhere but on the debate. It's spinning so fast I can't hear anything Audrey is saying. It's like she's talking underwater.

My hands start to shake. I look around the room. Faces swim toward me, then recede, like those dreams I used to have when I was little and way overtired.

I'm losing it.

A thin sheen of sweat breaks out along my upper lip. Beside me, Audrey finishes speaking. She rocked her part. She always does. Now she's ready for me to bring it home.

Patterson, the last member of the opposition, starts up. I've only got a few more seconds to pull my brain together so I can seal this thing and bring it to a close. But I feel like I need to…write.

Of course. What else?

My fingers seek out my pen, but I can't seem to find it. It's not here. It must have fallen off with the folder, and now it's on the floor somewhere.

Beside the podium, where no one can see, Audrey gently rests her hand on my arm. She doesn't look at me. But I know she's sending me her vibes.

Her touch brings me back. I draw in a deep breath and hold it. Then I let it out slowly. I feel dizzy.

Audrey squeezes.

You can do this.

But then, like the guy in the horror movie who can't stop walking toward the dark cellar door, my eyes search the audience. Looking for him. Needing to take the final step in this march of disgrace. Needing to know what he thinks of me.

When I find him, I realize he's been waiting for me. Our eyes lock. But where I expect to find disappointment and contempt, I find something else. It's…

I don't know what it is.

It's confusing.

Patterson stops speaking and the room falls silent again. All eyes turn my way.

I'm up.

I take a breath and straighten my spine.

"Thank you for your words, Honorable Member Patterson," I say. The words issue from me like the well-rehearsed preamble they are. A bit of composure surges back.

"I would like to take the opportunity to thank you

all for coming today," I say, glancing around. I make warm eye contact with a few audience members. This is a bit off the script, but nothing outside the lines. I'm just tweaking it a little. Building back my persona.

I look toward the judges, opening my folder as I do so. I went to the trouble of picking all that paper up. I might as well use it.

"Honorable judges, I hope to leave you with a few thoughts that will carry over past our debate here this afternoon."

Beside me, Audrey relaxes.

Chick is in the house.

I glance down at my notes.

And my breath disappears.

And...every word of my closing argument disappears with it.

I stare down at the page in front of me. At the sheet of paper that somehow must have been gathered up along with my debate notes at the last, hurried second when I was leaving my room.

Things I'm Dying to Say to My Dad

I blink once. Twice. Harder. But it's still there. The whole damn list.

The audience is silent, waiting. The room is so quiet you could hear a mosquito scratch its butt. Everyone is waiting for me to finish this thing. Wrap it up, hammer it down, pull it in, bring it home.

And I can't remember a single thing I was planning to say.

Audrey shifts a little, then glances at me. She looks at my notes, perhaps thinking she can take over and salvage what's left.

But she can't.

Her eyes widen when she sees what's in front of me. She looks back at my face.

But I'm looking at my dad.

And all of a sweet sudden, I know exactly what I'm going to say.

I clear my throat. What the hell. He wants to learn how to be a better listener, right?

"Things I'm Dying to Say to…Someone Who Needs to Hear Them: A List," I begin. "By Tadeusz Yosef Goldstein."

Out of the corner of my eye, I see Mr. Chadderton sit up in his chair. He doesn't like surprises.

"Number one," I say before I can chicken out. "You don't control my life. *I* control my life."

My voice shakes a little, but I keep my volume high and my words slow.

"Number two. I am not here on earth to make up for your mistakes, or to do the things you missed out on."

A murmur of confusion rises from the audience. I don't look up. I can't. Not yet.

"Number three. Winning is not the most important thing to me. Also known as: I actually *like* to pass the ball."

The murmuring grows. Audrey's hand squeezes me again, an invisible high five.

I take a deep, steadying breath. I glance up. Mr. Chadderton makes a cutting motion at his throat. His eyes are bugging out of his head.

But I'm not stopping. Gary, Johnna and Randy are staring at me like I've sprouted pink hooves and a mane. Iyengar is nodding like he's heard it all before.

I look down.

"Number four. I don't want to be a lawyer. Of any sort. Ever." The noise in the audience has died down. People are actually listening. I risk another glance up, but not in his direction. An older woman dressed in red throws me a thumbs-up.

As Mr. Chadderton makes his way toward the judges' table, I take another deep breath. I'm not going to make it through all ten. But there's one I am absolutely not going to miss.

"Number five. I don't want to be in Debate Club after this term. I want to do screenwriting."

Far in the back, someone hoots. It breaks the spell I'm under, and fear rushes back in.

I grip the sides of the podium fiercely. "Yeah," I nod, squinting in the direction of the voice.

My vision starts to swim a little. I look for him then, and when I see him, I take him square on. Straight in the eye. I can't read his expression. But— almost to my disbelief—he nods. It's slow. More a dip of the chin than a nod.

But it's there.

And it gives me the strangest feeling. Like I'm being put back together somehow.

I clear my throat. "Honorable judges," I say, forcing my gaze back to the adjudication table. "I would like to apologize for interrupting what has been an otherwise reasonable debate with my personal agenda." I shrug helplessly. "But sometimes a guy's gotta vent."

A ripple of laughter courses through the audience.

I bring my attention back to finishing my closing arguments. I wrap it up quickly and nod my thanks, and then Audrey and I shake hands with our opponents.

Mr. Chadderton flutters around the adjudication table as the judges make their notes. I guess I've blown our chances for regionals.

Doesn't matter to me, because I'm not going.

As the applause dies away and people start to move around, I look up, into the audience. My parents are gone, likely on their way out to the foyer for the intermission, where they'll wait for me while the judges make their final decisions. And anyway, I'm sure Dad wasn't exactly keen to stick around after my subjecting him to a public blasting.

Later there will be explaining to do, some sorting and talking. Maybe even some rearranging.

And hopefully some changing.

I turn to Audrey and draw an imaginary sword. She bows, and I throw it to her. She catches it, grins and then raises it high.

Iyengar looks our way. "You guys are on catnip or something," he says. "I've never seen anyone add a twist like that at the end, Goldstein."

I shrug. "Wasn't in the script."

"Well, whatever it was, it was well said." He nods.

"Thanks."

"The funny thing is, you'll probably still win."

"God, I hope not."

He laughs, and the three of us push through the double exit doors. The daylight is blinding, and I squint.

"Chick."

I turn toward the sound of my name. And he's there, looking at me like he's never really seen me properly before. But he's trying to now.

I drop my folder into the trash can in the foyer and grin.

I feel free.

Alex Van Tol is the author of many books for kids and teens, including *Great Bear Rainforest: A Giant-Screen Adventure in the Land of the Spirit Bear* with Ian McAllister and several titles in the Orca Currents, Soundings and Sports lines. Alex lives in Victoria, British Columbia, with her family.